What was that?

...e investigating the saw
...nd hadn't heard it.

"OO-OO-OO." The soft hooting
...med to be coming from among the
...nches of the fallen tree. She pulled
...m aside. The wood scratched her hands
...t she took no notice.

Emily caught her breath. A pair of
...rrified brown eyes stared up at her.
A young orang-utan was cowering in
...he tree!

Meet all of Emily's
WILD FRIENDS

WILD FRIENDS

ORANG-UTAN ADVENTURE

By Linda Chapman and Michelle Misra

Illustrated by Rob McPhillips

RED FOX

WWF WILD FRIENDS: ORANG-UTAN ADVENTURE

A RED FOX BOOK 978 1 849 41695 5

First Published in Great Britain by Red Fox,
an imprint of Random House Children's Publishers UK
A Random House Group Company

This edition published 2013

1 3 5 7 9 10 8 6 4 2

Random House Children's Publishers UK uses the WWF marks under license from
WWF–World Wide Fund for Nature. WWF is not the manufacturer of this product.

WWF-UK is a charity reg'd in England and Wales (no. 1081247) and in Scotland
(no. SC039593) and relies on support from its members and the public. This product is
produced under license from WWF-UK (World Wide Fund for Nature) Trading Limited,
Godalming, Surrey, GU7 1XR. Thank you for your help.

The Random House Group Limited supports the Forest Stewardship Council® (FSC®), the
leading international forest-certification organisation. Our books carrying the FSC label are
printed on FSC®-certified paper. FSC is the only forest-certification scheme supported by the
leading environmental organisations, including Greenpeace. Our paper procurement policy can
be found at www.randomhouse.co.uk/environment

Set in Bembo MT
Red Fox Books are published by Random House Children's Publishers UK,
61–63 Uxbridge Road, London W5 5SA

www.**randomhousechildrens**.co.uk
www.**randomhouse**.co.uk

Addresses for companies within The Random House Group Limited
can be found at: www.randomhouse.co.uk/offices.htm

THE RANDOM HOUSE GROUP Limited Reg. No. 954009

A CIP catalogue record for this book is available from the British Library.

Printed and bound by CPI Group (UK) Ltd, Croydon, CR0 4YY

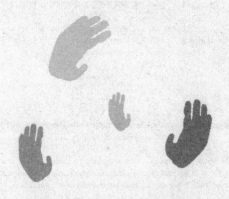

Turn to page 77 for lots of information on WWF, plus some cool activities!

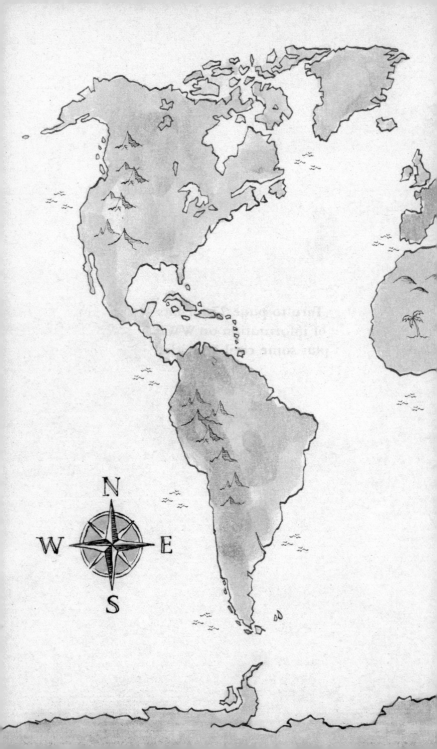

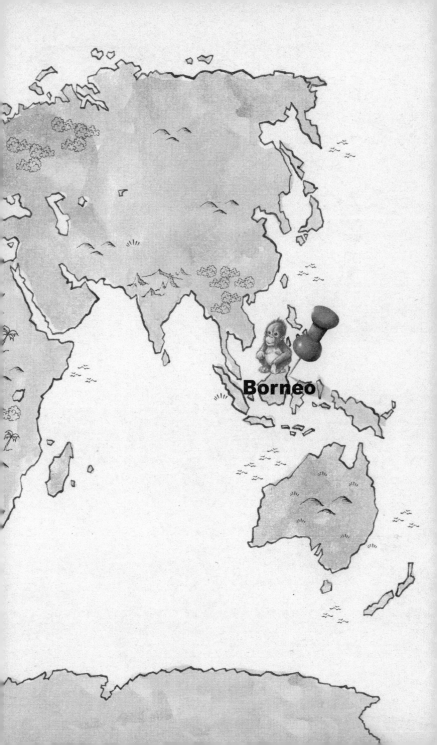

Borneo

Caught ⊙n Camera!

"Smile!" Emily Oliver called to her best friend Molly, who was sitting under a tree in the park.

Molly rolled her eyes. "Stop taking photos of me! You've got loads already."

"So?" said Emily, clicking the button on her new camera anyway. "I've got to practise taking photos before I go away next week."

The following week Emily and her parents were going to Borneo to see orang-utans in the wild. Emily's mum and dad both worked for WWF, an organization

that tried to protect endangered animals
and their habitats around the world. Emily's
mum had given her a camera of her own so
she could take photos while they were there.

"I wish you could come with me," Emily
sighed.

"Me too," Molly said. "But at least I get
to look after Cherry while you're away!"

Cherry was Emily's chinchilla. Usually
the people next door looked after her when
Emily and her parents were away on their
travels, but this time Molly's parents had

said she could look after the chinchilla.

"You do know all the things she likes, don't you?" said Emily anxiously. She hated leaving her pet. "Carrots and dried apple chunks for treats."

"I know," said Molly. "And she loves raisins but can't have too many of them. She can have as many cuddles as she wants, though. She'll be fine with me, Em. I promise I'll look after her really well."

"Thanks," Emily said, smiling. "I know she'll love being with you."

"So why are your parents going to Borneo?" Molly asked.

"Well, Mum's going to take photos," said Emily. Her mum was a wildlife photographer. "And Dad is checking up on a project there that he's been looking after. It monitors the number of orang-utans in the forest where we're going." She remembered some of the things she had been reading about orang-utans in the last few days. "Did you know that orang-utans are one of the most intelligent animals in the world? They use tools and build nests for themselves."

"Nests?" said Molly in surprise. "They're not birds!"

"No, but they do sleep in trees, just like birds do," said Emily. "They can build a new nest in just five minutes and they have really long arms, up to two metres."

"Wow!" said Molly, looking at her own arms. "That's mega-long!"

Emily grinned. "The adult males are eight times as strong as humans, too. Just imagine that! The babies are really cute though." She pictured some of the orang-utans she had seen on the Internet. The adults were covered with long, shaggy red-brown hair, the colour of a conker fresh out of its shell. They had dark grey faces, big brown eyes and mouths that could smile or look sad. The babies were like the adults but their fur was less thick and their eyes looked massive in their little faces. "They make an OO-OO-OO noise."

Molly copied her.

"That's right," said Emily. "It's quiet when they're scared and loud when they're excited."

"So what do orang-utans do all day?" asked Molly curiously.

"Eat, mainly!" said Emily. "They love fruit and eat lots of it. But they also eat bark and seeds and insects. When they're not eating they swing through the trees from their arms."

"I can do that!" Molly grinned and jumped up. The oak tree had a sturdy branch just above her head. She jumped up and caught hold of it and then swung herself back and forward. "I'm an orang-utan!"

she shouted as she hung from one arm.

Emily grinned and snapped a quick photo. "I'll show the orang-utans this and tell them I've found them a long lost cousin of theirs!"

Molly giggled and switched to the other arm. "OO-OO-OO!"

Shoving her camera in the pocket of her jeans, Emily jumped up and grabbed the branch too. "Come on, let's play at being orang-utans!"

She swung after her friend, happiness bubbling through her. Playing with Molly was great fun but soon she would be seeing orang-utans for real!

Into the Rainforest

The days seemed to drag by until it was time to go to Borneo, but at last Emily was on the plane. It was a long journey and, after they landed and got through customs, they had to travel by jeep for several hours. The sun had started to set by the time they reached their destination – an entrance into the heart of the rainforest. A research assistant on the orang-utan project was waiting to meet them. She was in her twenties with light brown hair tied back in a ponytail.

"Hi! My name's Rebecca," she greeted

them as they got out of the jeep.

Emily stretched. Her muscles felt stiff from all the travelling. The air in the rainforest was hot and damp and the buzz and hum of insects filled the air. In the trees around her she could hear birds and monkeys calling and whooping. It was amazing to be there!

"Hi, Rebecca," Mrs Oliver said, shaking hands with the research assistant. "It's lovely to meet you at last. You obviously know

Mike from his last trip here, and this is our daughter, Emily."

Rebecca shook hands with them all. "How was the journey?"

As the adults talked and the driver unloaded their rucksacks, Emily wandered over to the trees. Everywhere was so green! The tree trunks reared up high into the sky, long creepers fell from their branches and water dripped from the leaves.

"It's a fantastic place, isn't it?" Rebecca said, joining her. "Have you ever been to the rainforest before?"

"No," said Emily, swatting away a mosquito that was buzzing around her head.

"Well, there'll be lots for you to see. I'll show you all to the base where we stay and then you can unpack. Tomorrow we'll go out looking for orang-utans."

"Sounds great!" Mr Oliver said.

Mrs Oliver picked up her rucksack and heaved it onto her back. "Are you ready to go exploring then, Em?"

"Oh yes!" Emily breathed.

They set off down a track that twisted its
way through the trees. Emily stared around.
"Look!" she gasped as a troop of creamy
light brown monkeys swung through the
branches ahead.

"They're macaque monkeys," Rebecca
said. "You'll see lots of them in
the forest. Look over there!"
She pointed out a large
black and white bird
with a massive curved
yellow beak hopping

along a fallen tree trunk.

"That's a hornbill, isn't it?" Mr Oliver said.

Rebecca nodded. "There are more than four hundred different species of resident birds in Borneo. It's a bird lover's paradise."

"It's a paradise full stop," Mrs Oliver said, looking around happily.

Emily nodded in agreement. Her skin was damp with sweat, and branches and creepers grabbed at her feet and arms, but she didn't care. There was so much to see!

"I'm not sure about paradise. There are bad things about the rainforest too," said Rebecca with a laugh. "Mosquitos, for a start." She swatted away a couple from around her head. "And leeches. You also have to watch out for scorpions and poisonous snakes."

Emily didn't care about the dangers. "Will we see any orang-utans near here?" she asked eagerly.

"Probably not, they're not usually in this part of the forest," said Rebecca. "But hopefully we'll see lots tomorrow when we go deeper into the trees."

"How's the project going?" asked Mrs Oliver. "What are the numbers of orang-utans like?"

Rebecca tightened her ponytail. "Not great. Unfortunately there has been a lot of deforestation in this area and that's really affected the number of orang-utans."

"What's deforestation?" Emily asked.

"It's when trees in the rainforest are cut down, either to be used as timber, or to make areas where people can plant crops – or, in this area, oil palm plantations," Rebecca explained.

"When the trees are cut down the orang-utans suffer," Emily's dad added. "They don't have the shelter or the food they need."

"Recently, the number of orang-utans here has reduced dramatically. In the last fifty years the population has halved," said Rebecca. "Orang-utans only live in the wild here in Borneo or in a place called Sumatra, so it's really worrying that the number has fallen so much. The government has stepped in now and is trying to control the cutting down of trees

to help the orang-utans, and we inform the
authorities if we find any illegal logging –
trees being cut down for timber, that kind of
thing – but the forest is so big, it's impossible
to keep track of everything that is going on.
Even with deforestation being more tightly
controlled, the number of orang-utans is
not increasing very quickly. Orang-utans
don't have babies very often, you see, so the
population is going to take a long time to
recover."

Emily frowned. "Why
didn't people stop the
deforestation sooner?"
she asked. She couldn't
understand how people
could possibly cut trees down if it meant
endangering orang-utans – and other
animals who lived in the forest too.

"Unfortunately there's a lot of money
to be made from timber and oil palm

plantations," Mr Oliver explained. "So the companies who were cutting the trees down didn't want to stop."

"At least something is being done now," said Mrs Oliver. "I just hope it's not too late. It would be awful if the only orang-utans were in zoos or nature reserves. They're meant to live wild in the forest."

"The word orang-utan actually means 'man of the forest', and you're right," Rebecca said to Mrs Oliver. "It would be a tragedy if the wild orang-utans were wiped out. We're doing all we can to help them increase in numbers."

"Will we see any babies?" Emily asked.

"I can't promise that, but you might be lucky!" said Rebecca. "Some of the females do have babies at the moment – both newborn babies and youngsters. Baby orang-utans live with their mothers for a long time – they don't start going off on their own until they are four or five years old and they often carry on living with their mothers until they are older."

They reached a fork in the track. "The base is this way," Rebecca said, pointing to the left. "We're almost there now. Not too much further to walk!"

The WWF base was a cluster of wooden lodges and huts on stilts built in a clearing

beside a river. It was a simple place where the researchers could live and have easy access to the forest. Washing was hanging up on lines and there were a couple of hammocks strung up between trees.

"You'll be staying in this hut," Rebecca said, showing the Olivers to a hut with three beds inside, each covered by a mosquito net hung from a circular

metal ring in the ceiling. The windows were large and had no glass in them. "The toilets are in that shed over there," she added, pointing to a hut by the river. "The shower block is next to it. We all eat together in the main lodge, that big building. Why don't you unpack and then come along and find me in the main lodge? I'll introduce you to the rest of the team."

Emily and her parents quickly emptied out their rucksacks. There was a jug and bowl of water for washing in and a small mirror on the wall. Emily gave her hair a quick brush and changed into a clean T-shirt.

"Let's go and meet everyone," her mum said.

They went to the main lodge. There was a verandah all around it and inside there was a sitting area with a large table, a workroom with computers and

a kitchen. Three people were sitting with
Rebecca. There was a bearded vet from
New Zealand called Tom, another research
assistant called Mai Lin and the head of the
research team, an older lady called Yvonne.
They all welcomed the Olivers warmly.

"Do sit down," Yvonne said. "You must
be worn out after all your travelling. Shinta,
our cook, has prepared supper."

"Here, have a drink of guava juice," said

19

Tom, pouring out glasses of a sweet pink juice from a jug on the table. "So how do you like the rainforest so far, Emily?"

"I love it," said Emily, pushing back her hair. "But it's very hot!"

They all laughed. "You get used to it," Yvonne reassured her.

"And it'll get cooler now the sun has set," said Tom. "But make sure you sleep under your mosquito net tonight. You don't want to be a feast for all the insects that are here!"

Emily could smell food cooking in the kitchen. She wondered what they would be having for supper. She'd once watched a TV programme about Borneo and had seen people eating big white grubs like massive maggots. She hoped they wouldn't be having those for tea!

She needn't have worried. Shinta, the cook, served a delicious dish of fresh fish from the river, cooked in bamboo with rice and noodles and lots of vegetables. By the time Emily had finished eating, she was falling asleep at the table.

"Bed for you," her dad said, noticing her eyelids closing. For once, Emily didn't object. She got to her feet sleepily. "Thank you for supper," she said. "It was delicious."

The adults smiled.

"Sleep well. Tomorrow we'll get up bright and early and head up the river to see the orang-utans!" said Rebecca.

Emily sighed happily. She couldn't wait!

Setting Off on an Adventure!

Emily was woken up by light streaming in through the windows. Birds were warbling outside, frogs were chirping and monkeys were hooting to each other. She sat up. "Mum! Dad!" she said, pushing back the mosquito net and wriggling out of her sleeping bag. "Wake up! It's morning!"

Her parents sighed and turned over in bed. "It's too early," said her mum.

"It's never too early!" said Emily. She felt much better after her night's sleep and padded across the wooden floor to the window. A dark brown deer was grazing

near to the huts.
She watched its ears
flicking, its head
lifting as it looked
around before
pulling up a few
quick mouthfuls of

grass. Rebecca came
down the steps of her hut and the deer
immediately bounded off into the trees.
Emily started to pull her clothes on. She
didn't want to waste time inside when there
was a rainforest waiting to be explored!

"Come on! Get up!" she urged her parents.

Her dad yawned. "All right, all right."

They all got dressed and then went to
the main lodge. They had coconut bread
and a platter of fresh fruit – pineapple,
melon and something pink called dragon
fruit – for breakfast, as well as more guava
juice to drink. It was a delicious meal but

Emily was impatient to be off.

At long last, the adults got up from the breakfast table and they all headed down to the river bank where there was a motorized kayak, which was a big kind of canoe.

"Have you got your camera?" Mrs Oliver asked Emily.

Emily nodded.

They all put on orange life jackets and piled into the kayak. Tom started the engine and they set off up the river. Emily felt a thrill of excitement. Travelling in a boat

made it feel like even more of an adventure!

The chug of the little engine blended in with the humming and whirring of the insects all around them. Trees lined the river, their branches dipping down into the water. As they motored up the river, they saw a massive white stork-like bird picking its way across a muddy bank on stick-thin legs. Tom stopped the boat so Emily and her mum could get some pictures and then they carried on.

Eventually Tom steered the kayak into a small bay and they got out, their feet sinking into the mud.

"The orang-utans can usually be found in this area," said Rebecca. "Keep an eye on

the tree canopy and see if you can spot any sitting in the branches or swinging through the trees. We've got a watchtower and that's a great place to see them from. We'll head that way. Keep your eyes peeled!"

They headed up a small path. Tree roots jutted out of the path and they had to push aside the large leaves of the bushes and plants that sprang out across the track. Emily could feel the air starting to heat up as the sun rose in the sky. Her hair prickled with sweat. When would they see an orang-utan?

Suddenly Rebecca stopped. "There!" she said softly. "High up in the fork of the trunk."

Emily followed her gaze. The leaves above them were shaking. Then she saw an orang-utan's shaggy red-brown back! It was stripping the fruit from the branches and stuffing them into its mouth. She put

her camera to her eyes
and zoomed in until
she could see the
orang-utan's dark
grey face and
huge hands and
feet.

"Is it a male or a
female?" she breathed.

"A female," said Tom,
looking through his binoculars. "She's too
small to be a male."

She didn't look small to Emily! As they
watched, the orang-utan took hold of the
branch and swung in a leisurely way to the
next tree. She looked so big and hairy and
strong but also strangely graceful. Emily
took more pictures with her camera. Her
mum was clicking away too.

"Let's leave her in peace now," said
Rebecca.

They continued on through the trees
and came across two mother orang-utans
and two youngsters. The two mothers sat
in a tree eating fruit and throwing down
the peel while the two youngsters swung
through the trees together.

"They're holding hands!" Emily realized.
"Look, Mum!"

"It's called buddying, isn't it, Rebecca?"
Mrs Oliver said.

Rebecca nodded. "When baby orang-
utans get old enough to climb on their

own, they usually team up with another youngster. They help each other through the trees."

Emily stared, entranced, as the two orang-utans swung about. It was like watching two little children at school – they pulled each other along and caught each other if their grip slipped. She'd never seen anything like it. They were so human! It was their eyes she particularly loved. They were big and dark brown, full of intelligence and a little hint of mischief.

The orang-utans swung on and Rebecca led the way towards the watchtower. They saw a brightly coloured kingfisher and a small glittering snake, but they didn't see any more orang-utans.

After a while, they reached a large clearing. Rebecca and Tom frowned. "That's not right," said Rebecca. "It looks as though over fifty trees have been cut down since we were last here."

Emily realized she was right. She could
see the stumps sticking out of the ground,
the freshly cut wood a pale creamy colour.

"This doesn't look good," said her dad,
walking forward to investigate. "People
have obviously been here – and recently
too. Look, you can see the footprints where
they've dragged the tree trunks they've
cut down to the river." He made his way
around the fallen tree and pointed out

tracks through the vegetation and in the mud of the river bank.

"Loggers," said Mrs Oliver. "People cutting trees down and selling them for timber." Suddenly there was a creaking, cracking noise from behind them. "What's that?" she said in alarm as birds around the clearing started squawking in alarm.

"Look!" gasped Rebecca as one of the trees started to slowly fall to one side. As they watched, it keeled over completely and with a loud crashing sound, it fell to the ground. Birds shot into the sky. Leaves and branches exploded upwards and for a moment the whole clearing seemed to shake with the impact of the crash.

Mrs Oliver stared in shock. "What happened there?"

As the crash faded away, Mr Oliver and Tom ran over to the tree trunk. "It's been cut half through with a chainsaw!" said Emily's dad, pointing out saw marks at the base. He looked grim.

"We could have been killed if it had fallen on us," said Rebecca, her face pale.

Mr Oliver frowned. "The people who did this must be stopped."

Emily walked around the fallen tree. There were swarms of insects buzzing frantically in the air and birds circling overhead, their nests suddenly demolished. Poor things. Thank goodness there hadn't been any animals in the branches or underneath the tree when it fell ...

"OO-OO-OO ... OO-OO-OO ..."

Emily stiffened as she heard a small scared hooting noise. What was that?

The adults were investigating the saw marks and hadn't heard it.

"OO-OO-OO." The soft hooting seemed to be coming from among the branches of the fallen tree. She pulled them aside. The wood scratched her hands but she took no notice.

Emily caught her breath. A pair of terrified brown eyes stared up at her. A young orang-utan was cowering in the tree!

A New Friend

The young orang-utan huddled down
among the leaves, its long arms wrapped
around its body. It rocked from side to side,
hooting in distress. Seeing Emily, it covered
its eyes with its hand as if it believed that
because it couldn't see her, she couldn't
see it. Emily's heart went out to the poor
frightened creature.

"OO-OO-OO," she mimicked softly.
The baby stopped rocking and peeped out
from under his arm. Emily made the noise
again and held out her hand.

The baby stared at her hand and then

at her face. "OO?" This time the sound was less scared and more questioning.

"OO," Emily said in reply.

Slowly the orang-utan reached out and grasped her hand. She felt its warm fingers close around her own and looked into its eyes. It stared back at her. "Hello," Emily said softly.

"Em, what are you doing?" Mrs Oliver called.

Emily didn't want to frighten the baby so she didn't say anything.

"Emily?" Mrs Oliver repeated, walking over. "What are you . . . Oh my goodness!"

she gasped as she saw the orang-utan.

"It's all right. I just found him in the fallen tree," Emily whispered as the baby carried on gripping her finger. "He must have been in the branches when it fell."

"Wait there!" Mrs Oliver hurried to get the others.

Tom was beside Emily in an instant. He studied the baby. "He looks to be about two years old," he said. "I need to check he's not hurt." He reached towards the baby but the poor little creature shrank back in fear.

Tom moved back. "He's scared of me. He seems to like you though, Emily. I guess it's because you're smaller and female. Can you persuade him out?"

"I can try," Emily said.

The adults backed off. Emily talked softly to the baby. He edged closer to her. She held out her hand again. But this time the orang-utan didn't grasp her finger

– he leaped straight into her arms! He
was heavy, about the weight of a large
human toddler, and Emily gave a squeak
of surprise, staggering slightly as the baby
clung to her shoulders. The orang-utan
looked up into her face.

"It's OK," she soothed the baby. "Don't
worry. There's nothing to be scared of." Her
arms folded around him and in spite of his
weight, she was able to rock him slightly

like a human baby. Soon she felt him relax.

"Good girl," Tom told her softly. "You're doing great. He seems to have decided you're a substitute mum. See if you can move away from the tree and sit down with him. He might start to relax and let me check him over."

Emily carried the baby over to one of the tree stumps. She could feel his little heart beating and the warmth of his body as he clung to her like a limpet to a rock.

Emily sat down on the tree stump and the adults crouched around her. Gradually the orang-utan sat back in her lap and then touched her cheek with his hand. She smiled at him. "Hello." His eyes glinted and he reached around to suddenly tug her ponytail.

Emily giggled. "Stop it!"

Her laugh seemed to relax the baby even more. He turned to look curiously at the adults. Mrs Oliver was taking loads of photos with one of her big cameras.

"Isn't he cute?" said Emily's dad as the orang-utan baby stared around at them all.

Tom moved over quietly and started stroking him too. Now the baby had relaxed, he accepted the vet checking him over. Tom pulled out his phone and read some notes.

"Is he all right?" Emily asked, stroking the baby.

"Yes, he seems fine," said Tom. "He's one of the babies we've been monitoring. I recognize him by the tuft of hair on his right ear that sticks up. I've got his notes on my phone. He's called Koyah and he's two years old."

Rebecca was nodding. "We usually see him with his mum, Sami." Emily saw the worry in her eyes. "I wonder where she is. I've never known them to be apart. Koyah hasn't started buddy travelling like the other orang-utans his age. He always travels with Sami. We've noted that he seems to lack confidence."

An alarming thought struck Emily. "Do you think the people who cut the trees down might have taken his mum?"

Tom frowned. "Poachers have been known to take orang-utans and sell them as pets. They can get quite a lot of money for them, but they would normally take a baby rather than an adult."

"Then maybe she was hurt by the tree falling," Emily said anxiously.

"I think we'd have seen her or heard her," said Tom.

"It's more likely she was frightened off

and jumped out of the tree," said Mr Oliver, looking around him. "She'd have probably been expecting Koyah here to follow her, but if he isn't confident about travelling around he might have been too frightened when the tree started to fall."

"So what do we do?" said Mrs Oliver, putting the lens cover on her camera and coming over. "Do we take him back to the base camp? And what about the loggers? If they come back they're likely to endanger more orang-utans if they start chopping down more trees."

"We mustn't take Koyah away from here in case his mum comes back," said Tom. "But we do need to tell Yvonne and Mai Lin about the loggers and work out what to do."

"Maybe some of us should go back and some stay—" Emily's dad started to say. He broke off as a loud long hoot echoed

across the clearing: "OOOOOOOO!"
It rang out again. "OOOOOOOO!"

"It's Sami – Koyah's mum!" said
Rebecca as an adult orang-utan came
swinging quickly through the trees and
dropped to the ground in the clearing.
"Look!"

Koyah had stiffened in delight at the
sound of his mum's call. He leaped from
Emily. She watched as he ran across the
grass on all fours and jumped into his
mother's waiting arms, bowling her over
onto her back.

Sami hugged
her baby tightly.
She rocked him
from side to side
as if she was a
human mum
who had just
found her missing

toddler. Then she sat up and he snuggled
into her shaggy chestnut fur.

Emily sighed in relief. She had loved
cuddling Koyah but she was very glad his
mum had come back.

Sami turned and walked towards the
trunk of the nearest tree with Koyah beside
her. She swung her way up the trunk.

Koyah followed her, his strong, agile hands
and feet gripping the bark. Emily felt a bit
sad she hadn't had a chance to say goodbye
but it was great to see him with his mum
again.

Mrs Oliver hugged Emily. "I'm so glad Sami is OK."

"Me too," Emily said.

"The question now is how we keep them safe," said Mr Oliver. "Neither of them were hurt this time, but if the loggers return they may not be so lucky."

"We have to do something to stop the loggers!" said Emily. She looked at the river bank. "They must have left just before we got here. We should go after them!"

"Whoa, Em!" her dad said. "We can't just go haring off up the river. We need to go back to base camp and think up a plan of action like Tom said."

The vet nodded. "Let's go back and tell the others what we've found here and then we can decide what to do."

45

Emily followed the adults back through the trees towards the kayak. She could see the logic in going back to the base camp, but worry was gnawing through her. What if the loggers came back while they were gone? What if Koyah and Sami or any of the other orang-utans were killed or caught and taken away? Emily felt sick. *Oh please,* she prayed, *please let the loggers stay away and the orang-utans be all right.*

Lost!

Back at the base, the team sat around the table and tried to work out the best thing to do. "We need to catch the loggers in the act," said Yvonne. "The authorities won't be able to do anything until we have some evidence of who the loggers are."

"But catching them isn't going to be easy," said Tom. "We've no idea where they'll strike next."

"Yes, but Yvonne's right. There's nothing we can do unless we actually see them," Mr Oliver said.

Listening to all the talking, Emily felt

very frustrated. She wanted the adults to do something to stop the loggers for good. She hated the thought of the orang-utans – or any other animals – being in danger.

"I think I should probably go and have a look at what you found," said Yvonne.

"Heather and I will come back with you," said Mr Oliver, nodding over to his wife. "Heather can get some photos of the damage that's already been done."

Mrs Oliver nodded. "Good plan."

"What about me? Can I come too?" Emily asked eagerly.

Her mum agreed. "We'll go after lunch."

They had a quick lunch of chicken and fried rice and then set off in the kayak again with Yvonne and Rebecca.

They left the kayak in the same spot and set off down the path. While Emily's mum and dad went with Yvonne to examine the clearing and take photos, Rebecca

suggested she took Emily on through the
trees to the watchtower. It looked a bit like
a metal scaffolding tower but was built out
of wood and
was very tall.
There were
three separate
platforms on
it at different
levels, and
ladders to climb
up and down
between them.
The team used
it for watching
the orang-utans
in the treetops.

It was hard
work climbing
all the way
up to the top

platform in the heat, but it was worth it!
When Emily looked at the tops of the
trees waving around her, she felt almost
like she was an orang-utan herself! It gave
her a totally different view of the forest.
Everything seemed so small below. As she
looked down, a black squirrel scampered
around the edge of the tower railing.

"So what do you think?" Rebecca asked
her.

"It's amazing!" Emily smiled, taking photos of the squirrel.

"I love it up here," said Rebecca. "You can see so much more of the forest."

Emily took more photos of birds and monkeys in the trees. She kept looking out for orang-utans, but she didn't spot any.

"We should go back to the clearing and see how the others are getting on," Rebecca said after a while.

"Oh," Emily said, disappointed. She was having so much fun being so high up in the trees. "Can't we stay for a bit longer?"

"Well . . ." Rebecca thought for a moment. "You could always stay here. I'll head back to the clearing and then come back here with the others. I'm sure they will want to take some photos as well. How does that sound?"

"Great!" Emily beamed.

Rebecca climbed down and Emily sat back on the platform enjoying watching a flock of brightly coloured birds flying through the treetops. After a while some very strange looking monkeys came swinging through the trees towards her. They were quite large with golden coats, big pink noses and fat tummies. They were chattering loudly. Emily stared. Most monkeys were cute but these were really quite ugly, although their eyes were bright and sparkly. The monkeys swung down to the ground. Emily began to climb down the tower with her camera. She really wanted to take some pictures of them! But just as she reached the bottom of the tower the monkeys scampered off into the forest. Emily tried to follow them but they were much faster than she was and she only managed to get a few photos of their tails before they disappeared!

She was about to head back to the tower when a movement in the bushes caught her eye. It was a young leopard with big spots! It stared at her with big green eyes

and then it trotted away down the path, its mottled coat blending in with the shadows. Emily followed it eagerly.

The leopard reached a clearing and disappeared into the bushes with a flick of its long tail. Emily stopped, realizing she'd come quite a long way from the watchtower now. Which was the way back? She thought she'd just been walking in a straight line but there were two paths a little way behind her, one to the left and one to the right. Which one had she come along?

She set off down the left path but the

further she walked, the less sure she was that it was the right one. The canopy overhead was thick and the light was very dim here. There was a fallen tree ahead of her, covered with moss and creepers, that she was sure she hadn't seen on the way out. She retraced her steps but then seemed to take a wrong turning because she didn't get back to the clearing where she had finally lost sight of the leopard. The shadows seemed to be growing thicker and the path narrower.

Worry started to prickle through her.

Don't panic, she told herself, trying to be sensible. *Just walk back along the path the way*

you've come and try and find the clearing. She
turned around but the path just wound on
and on through the trees.

Finally she reached a fork. She stopped in
the gloom. Her heart was beating fast. She
had no idea which way to go. She was lost!
Lost in the rainforest!

"OO-OO-OO!"

She heard a familiar hooting noise. There
was a rustle of leaves overhead and Emily
turned to see an adult and a baby orang-
utan swinging towards her!

Emily spotted the tuft of hair sticking up
on the baby's left ear and saw the greeting
in the baby's eyes.

"Koyah!" she gasped.

His mother waited in the trees but he
dropped to the ground and ran over to her,
leaning on the knuckles of his hands. He
stood up and wrapped his arms around her
knees. Emily crouched down and gave him

Take a look at some of the pictures that inspired this story

A young orang-utan swinging through the trees.

Orang-utans also live on the island of Sumatra.

Orang-utans spend most of their time in the treetops.

Baby orang-utans stay with their mum until they are 7 or 8 years old.

Orang-utan (Pongo pygmaeus) with child in a tree on a rehabilitation centre in Borneo, Malaysia. © Honing Heemskerk WWF -Netherlands

A mother orang-utan and her baby; just like Sami and Koyah.

This cute orang-utan looks just like Koyah!

a hug. "Oh, Koyah. I'm lost." She stroked his fluffy orange fur and kissed his head, feeling a bit better now he was there. If only he could tell her the way home.

Koyah touched her cheek with his hand and then turned and ran to the right fork. Emily hesitated. Maybe he would go to the clearing where she had first seen him and his mum?

She set off after him. He ran ahead of her down the path with his mum swinging above through the trees and calling down soft hoots. He hooted back, as if reassuring her, and then looked back at Emily. He seemed happy that she was following. After a little way, he swung up a tree and

hung down from
a high branch
by one arm. He
held out his other
hand towards her,
as if wanting her
to take it. He was
high above her
head.

"I can't reach
you up there,"
Emily told him. "I
can't climb trees
like you."

Koyah waved his hand at her but there
was no way she could reach it, so he swung
on, glancing back at her as she hurried
along, trying not to trip on the tree roots
and creepers that snaked across the path.

Suddenly Emily heard a noise. It was
a high-pitched whining sound and it was

coming through the trees to the left. It wasn't a noise made by an animal, she was sure about that. It sounded like a machine!

Koyah had heard it too. He stiffened and the next second bolted back through the trees towards his mum. Emily hesitated but pushed through the trees towards the sound. The noise was getting louder and louder and then suddenly there was a yell and a loud crash, just like when the tree had fallen before.

Emily froze. Someone was cutting trees down just a few metres away! It must be the illegal loggers!

She hesitated, torn between wanting to run away and wanting to go on and see the people responsible. She looked back at the orang-utans, the scared baby huddling beside his mum who had her arm around him. Seeing their sad eyes, Emily made an instant decision. She had to find out what

was going on. She would never forgive
herself if she did nothing and Koyah or his
mum got hurt. Taking a determined breath,
she crept on through the trees.

Hidden Camera

Emily crouched behind a bush and parted the large leaves. The noise of the chainsaw had started up again and was very loud in her ears, whining and screaming as the blade cut into a tree trunk. She peered between the leaves and saw a group of men near the river. Two of them had chainsaws and were cutting down the trees while clouds of birds flew around overhead, squawking and crying out.

Emily's heart thudded. What could she do? She wanted to rush out and stop the men but it was much too dangerous. If only her parents and the rest of the team were there, they could stop them. But she was on her own and lost. By the time she found her way back to the others, the men might have gone. She tried to fix pictures of them in her mind and then suddenly it dawned on her. Her camera! Of course! She didn't need to rely on her mind – she could take pictures of the men!

Taking her camera out of her pocket, she took photo after photo of the men cutting the

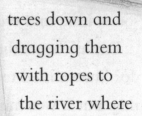

trees down and dragging them with ropes to the river where

a boat was waiting. She zoomed in on the men's faces. She didn't stop until she was sure she had captured the men from every angle, and a few close-ups of the boat they  were loading the timber into. Then she slowly let the leaves close and backed away. She retreated down the path to where Koyah and Sami were now sitting on a tree trunk. Koyah climbed up the trunk and began to swing from the branches, his mum following.

Emily hurried along the path. She didn't know where she was going but she knew she wanted to get as far away from the loggers as possible. The path twisted and

turned until she came out into a clearing. It
seemed familiar. Yes, there was the river and
the fallen tree! She was back where they
had first found Koyah!

She was sure the orang-utans had
brought her back here on purpose. She
could find the way back to the kayak from
here. "Oh, thank you!" she cried.

Suddenly she heard human voices.
Maybe it was the loggers come to find
more trees to cut down! She dived behind
a tree trunk.

"Emily! Emily! Where are you?"

It was her mum and Rebecca shouting her name!

"I'm here!" Emily cried, jumping out as her mum and Rebecca came hurrying along the path.

Both women jumped.

"Emily, where on earth have you been?" Mrs Oliver demanded, rushing over to her and sweeping her into a hug. "Everyone's looking for you."

"We were so worried when we got to the watchtower and found you'd disappeared!" Rebecca said.

"I'm sorry, I got lost," Emily said, relief rushing through her now she was back with her mum. "Mum, I saw the loggers! They're further up the river."

"You saw the loggers?" her mum gasped.

"Are you OK? Did they see you?" Rebecca asked anxiously.

"Yes, I'm fine, and no, they didn't see me."

"Can you remember what they looked like?" her mum said.

"Better than that." Emily grinned and pulled out her camera. "I've got photos of them right here!"

Her mum took the camera and quickly clicked through all the photographs Emily had just taken. "Em, these are brilliant," she said in astonishment. "They're concrete evidence of what these men are doing. The authorities will be able to use them to track them down. You've even zoomed in on their faces – and the logo on the side of the boat. That's obviously the company that's responsible. This is perfect!" She gave Emily another tight hug. "Oh, Em, this is just what we need to stop them!"

"So am I still in trouble for wandering off?" Emily asked.

Her mum smiled. "I think this once I'll forgive you." She fixed her with a stern look. "Just don't ever give me such a fright again. OK?"

"OK!" Emily agreed with relief.

The photos turned out to be just what the team were looking for. When Yvonne saw the photos she recognized some of the men immediately. Emily's mum printed the photos out and then Tom took them to the nearest town.

"The authorities are going to look into it straight away," Tom said when he got back to the base that evening. "The men you photographed have been suspected of logging before. Your photos will give the authorities the evidence they need to arrest them and charge them."

"So the forest will be safe again?" said Emily.

"It'll certainly be a lot safer," her dad said, squeezing her shoulder. "And that's thanks to you. You kept your head in a very frightening situation. I'm really proud of you, Em."

Emily blushed.

"And I'm really proud of your skills as a photographer," said her mum, clicking through the photos again on Emily's camera. "You've got some great shots here – not just of the loggers, but of the animals and birds you saw from the watchtower too. You're obviously a natural with the camera."

Emily's dad nudged her. "Maybe you'll follow in your mum's footsteps and be a wildlife photographer one day."

Emily glowed. She didn't know what she wanted to do when she grew up, but as long as it was something to do with wild animals she knew she'd be happy!

"I think we should celebrate with a night-time trek," said Tom, glancing outside into the gathering dark. "People say you haven't really seen the rainforest until you've seen it at night time. What do you think, Emily? Would you like that?"

"Oh, yes!" she breathed.

The night trek was incredible. It was slightly eerie to be walking into the darkness with just torches for light and creepers brushing against them, but there was so much to see. At night the forest was a completely different world. The air was cooler, there were brightly patterned frogs croaking on leaves and bats swooping around their heads. Emily spotted a

black bear disappearing into the trees and a cute bush baby perched in the fork of a tree, its eyes wide and luminous as it stared at them.

When they finally got back to the base, her head was filled with pictures of all the things she had seen. Shinta had a delicious supper of noodles and rice and chicken in ginger sauce ready for them. Afterwards, feeling full and happy, Emily sat on the sofa with her mum and dad and listened to the grown-ups sharing their animal adventures. It was the perfect evening.

"So do you like the rainforest?" her dad asked her as she snuggled against him.

"No." Emily saw her dad's surprised expression and grinned. "I don't just like it," she said. "I *love* it!"

Buddies

The next day, Emily and her parents headed to the watchtower again so Mrs Oliver could take some of her own shots from there. "I can't have you getting all the good photos!" she teased Emily.

Emily was more than happy to climb up to the top platform again and sit among the treetops with her dad while her mum took photo after photo.

"OO-OO-OO." Emily looked around as she heard a familiar noise. She grinned as she spotted Koyah swinging through the trees with another orang-utan.

"Koyah!" Emily blinked as she realized that the orang-utan he was with wasn't his mum, but another young orang-utan, about the same age as him. They were holding hands.

"Koyah's got a buddy, Dad! Look!" said Emily. "Rebecca said he's never had one before."

"Making friends with you must have helped him become more confident," her dad said. "Maybe it was just the little boost he needed."

Koyah swung onto the platform and ran
over to Emily. He hugged her knees and she
hugged him back. Then he flopped onto his
back, did a backward roly-poly and ran to
the edge of the platform where he re-joined
his little friend. They took hands. Koyah
gave Emily a cheeky grin and then swung
away through the trees.

Emily took out her own camera and
snapped a photo of the two orang-utan
friends. She couldn't wait to show it to
Molly when she got home. "They're just like

me and Molly when we
play at being orang-
utans in the park,"
she said happily
to her dad. As
she spoke, Koyah
swung himself
upside down from
a branch, holding on
with just his feet.

Her dad raised his eyebrows. "I hope
you're not planning on trying that! You've
given me enough grey hairs as it is on this
trip!"

Emily laughed. "Sorry, Dad."

Her dad watched the two young
orang-utans holding hands and put an arm
around her shoulder. "You know something,
though?"

"What?" Emily said.

"I wouldn't want to change a thing."

Mr Oliver kissed the top of her head and together they watched the two young orang-utans swing away through the trees.

Read on for lots of amazing orang-utan facts, fun puzzles and more about WWF

WWF

Orang-Utan Fact File

Best feature: Orang-utans are extremely clever and often make tools in the wild. They have been recorded making umbrellas and ponchos from leaves when it rains, using sticks to get honey out of beehives and using leaves as napkins and cushions!

Size: Males can be 1.5m tall and weigh as much as 120kg. Females are much smaller. They grow up to 1m tall and weigh about 45kg. They are the largest tree-climbing animals in the world.

Favourite food: Orang-utans are omnivores but 60%

of their diet is made up of fruit. Their favourites' are huge spiky fruits called Durian, these fruits smell very bad, and taste a bit like custard and garlic, but orang-utans love them! They also eat young leaves and shoots, honey, insects, tree bark, and occasionally eggs and small vertebrates.

Home: Orang-utans once lived in an area ranging from southern China to the foothills of the Himalayas and south to Java. Now they only survive in Indonesia and Malaysia on the islands of Borneo and Sumatra.

Current population: A century ago, there were around 230,000 orang-utans in Borneo and Sumatra and now only around 7,500 survive on Sumatra and 55,000 on Borneo.

Breeding and family: Orang-utans are not very sociable and do not live in groups. Female orang-utans often have one or two babies with them but male orang-utans usually live alone. When orang-utans are born they weigh about 3 ½ pounds. For the first two years of a young orang-utan's life, he or she is completely dependent on their mother for food and transportation. There is a lot to learn about life in the forest and so young orang-utans stay with their mother and learn from her until they are 7 or 8 years old. This is longer than any other mammal except humans.

Life span: In the wild, orang-utans may live up to 45 years or more. The oldest captive orang-utan was a male called "Guas" at the Philadelphia Zoo who lived until he was 58 years old!

Biggest threat: The most serious threat to orang-utans is the destruction of their rainforest habitat. Humans are responsible for this habitat loss as they cut down the trees to sell as timber or to make way for new farms and towns. Orang-utans are also in danger from poachers who kill them for their meat or capture the baby orang-utans to sell as pets.

Bonus fact: Almost every night orang-utans construct a new sleeping nest from branches, usually 15 to 100 feet up in a tree.

Quiz time!

1. What colour are orang-utans?

2. How old is Koyah?

3. What is an orang-utan's favourite food?

4. What animal does Emily follow down the path?

5. What is it called when two baby orang-utans pair up?

6. Where is Tom the vet from?

1: reddish-brown, 2 years old, fruit, a leopard, buddying, New Zealand

Word Search

Reading across, up, down and diagonally,
see if you can find all the listed words
in the grid below . . .

Q	E	R	P	O	R	L	V	B	D	B	E	N
X	T	B	D	C	S	O	X	Y	O	G	N	O
R	S	O	R	A	N	G	U	T	A	N	X	I
A	W	R	V	N	M	X	E	D	F	E	I	T
I	A	L	I	O	V	J	N	O	J	M	O	A
N	C	L	D	P	I	O	V	K	N	E	S	T
F	S	Z	V	Y	E	F	X	I	O	O	F	S
O	B	E	L	L	I	B	N	R	O	H	P	E
R	E	O	D	O	N	D	K	A	Y	D	N	R
E	M	N	R	I	X	O	V	I	Z	V	F	O
S	D	I	X	N	M	D	E	R	X	I	X	F
T	F	O	V	D	E	O	F	O	M	E	V	E
V	O	M	E	O	L	O	G	G	E	R	S	D

ORANG-UTAN	CANOPY	HORNBILL	RAINFOREST
BORNEO	DEFORESTATION	NEST	LOGGERS

Word Scramble

The names of these characters from the book are all jumbled up. Can you unscramble them?

CACBREE

☐☐☐☐☐☐☐

ILMINA

☐☐☐☐☐☐

ISMA

☐☐☐☐

NNYOVE

☐☐☐☐☐☐

OAKHY

☐☐☐☐☐

Story Jumble!

Can you put these parts of the story below
back in the order they happened?

A – Emily finds a baby orang-utan

B – Emily meets the WWF team

C – Emily takes photos of the loggers

D – Emily sees a leopard

Correct order

More about WWF

You're probably familiar with WWF's panda logo,
but did you know that WWF . . .

- Is the world's leading conservation organization.

- Was set up in 1961 (when TV was still black and white!).

- Works with lots of different people around the world, including governments, businesses and individuals, to make a difference to the world we live in.

- Is a charity and most of their money comes from members and supporters.

WWF's aim

The planet is our most precious resource and we need to take care of it! WWF want to build a future where people live in harmony with nature.

WWF are working towards this by:

Protecting the natural world.

Helping to limit climate change and find ways to help people deal with the impacts of it.

Helping to change the way we live, so that the world's natural resources (like water and trees) are used more carefully, so they last for future generations.

Borneo, Malaysia. © Honing Heemskerk /WWF -Netherlands

What do WWF do?

 Conservation – Protect rare species of wild animals and plants as well as important ecosystems found in forests, rivers and seas.

Climate change – They don't just tackle the causes of global warming, but also the impacts of climate change on communities and environments.

 Sustainability – Help to change the way we all live, particularly in richer developed countries like the UK, including decisions about what we eat, buy and use for fuel.

How can I help WWF?

There are lots of ways you can take action in your own home to help protect our beautiful planet and the people and animals that live on it. Here are a few ideas to get you started ...

Buy sustainable

One of the biggest threats to a lot of wildlife, including the giant panda, is loss of habitat. This is often from people cutting down trees to use in paper or wood products, or to make way for roads, and clearing areas to use for farming.

You can help stop this by only buying products that are sustainably farmed, or wood and paper products from sustainable forests.

So when you're out shopping with your mum or dad, look for:

- **Certified paper and wood products** (look for the FSC logo to tell if something is certified or not)

- **Products made from certified sustainable palm oil** (look for the RSPO logo to be sure that they are certified)

If your local shops don't stock these products – ask them why!

Reduce, reuse, recycle!

Households in the UK send 18 million tonnes of rubbish to landfill yearly. That's more than any other country in Europe!

Top five tips to reduce waste

Why don't you do some of these over a week and see how much less rubbish you throw away than normal?

Take a reuseable bag when you go to the shops, instead of picking up a new one.

Take any clothes, shoes, books or toys you don't want any more to a charity shop.

Clean out old food jars and pots to use for storage.

Get creative with your rubbish and make a kitchen-roll penguin.

Make postcards by cutting old birthday and Christmas cards in half, and give them to your friends.

"Go Wild!"

The way we live can affect people, wildlife and habitats all around the world. Making small but important changes to the way we act really can help to save polar bears in the Arctic or orang-utans in Borneo and Sumatra.

And this is what the Go Wild club is all about. It's your chance to learn more about some of the animals and habitats that we're working to protect. It's also about discovering what you can do in your own home to help look after the natural world.

By joining WWF's Go Wild club at *wwf.org.uk/gowildjoin*, you will recieve a member's pack and magazines that will take you on an incredible journey around the world, meeting some amazing animals and individuals. You'll find out what life's like for them and the threats they face to their environments.

As well as getting lots of Go Wild goodies, being a member means that you help WWF to continue their work. Join today and explore your wild side!

Don't miss Emily's adventure with her
very first wild friend, Kihari the elephant,
in ELEPHANTS NEVER FORGET.

Read on for a sneak peek!

One Week to Go

The rain poured. Emily Oliver sat by the window, watching the drops race each other down the glass pane. Outside, the world looked grey. All the animals and birds in the garden were sheltering in the trees. Emily could hardly believe that in just a week's time she would be in Kenya, a very hot country in Africa. Excitement tingled through her. Loads of different wild animals lived there – lions, giraffes, zebras, cheetahs, gazelle, buffalo – and best of all, *elephants*!

Emily loved all animals, but she particularly liked elephants with their wrinkly grey skin, big flapping ears and kind, wise eyes. *I wonder if I'll meet one,* she thought. She had been to all sorts of amazing places because her mum and dad worked for WWF, an organization that helped protect animals and their habitats around the world. Emily's mum was a photographer and her dad helped set up WWF projects in different countries. But this trip was different – this time they were going on holiday. And not just any holiday – on safari!

They were going to fly to the capital of Kenya, Nairobi, and then stay a night with one of her mum and dad's friends who worked for WWF, before travelling the next day to the Masai Mara Nature Reserve. It would take them a few hours by minibus to get there, but Emily didn't mind. She had never been on safari before and she couldn't wait!

She wandered around the room, feeling restless – she wished she was already in Kenya! Her eyes fell on a collection of photo albums on the bookcase. They were full of her mum's photos from around the world. All the covers were labelled and many of them were from before Emily had been born. As Emily began to look through them, she wondered if there were any with photos of Africa in them.

Australia . . . India . . . Russia . . . Her eyes skipped over the different labels and then saw one that said *Kenya*. She pulled it out of the pile and opened it up.

There were photos of her mum and dad

standing by a river full of hippos. They were with some other people and a toddler with dark curly hair in bunches. Emily frowned. It looked like her, but had she ever been to Kenya? She didn't think so. Still, she had definitely looked like that when she was a toddler.

She turned the page of the album and gasped out loud as she saw dozens of photos of elephants. There were elephants bathing at a watering hole, elephants spraying water over themselves, elephants twining trunks. And then she saw a close-up photo of a young elephant. It was touching the toddler's tummy with its trunk and she was touching its grey wrinkled

cheek. They were
gazing at each
other, completely
ignoring the
camera. The
toddler was
smiling and if
elephants could

smile, this one would have been smiling
back. Was it really her in the photo?

Just then the door opened and her mum
came in. "Gran's going to make a cake. She
said do you want to come and help her?"

"Look, Mum." Emily waved the photo
album at her. "I found these. Is this me?
Have I been to Kenya before?"

Her mum's dark hair was loose around
her shoulders. She tucked it behind her ears
as she looked at the photos. "Yes. You were
about two years old then." She smiled, as if
remembering. "It was your first big trip

abroad. I travelled out there to take some photos in the Masai Mara and you and Dad came with me. That was when we got to know Abasi, whose flat we'll be staying at this time. I'd forgotten you'd been there with us."

Emily pointed to the photo of the elephant tickling her tummy with its trunk. "Look at this!"

Her mum smiled fondly. "I remember that! Weren't you cute? That elephant had been orphaned and was really shy and reserved with people and other elephants, but she took a real shine to you. Maybe it was because you were so small. She used to call out to you and you would make a noise back. Then she'd follow you around and touch your hair and tickle your tummy with her trunk. You used to say she was a heffalant. I suppose you could say she was your very first wild friend."

Emily stared at the picture of the young elephant with intelligent eyes. She wished she could remember meeting her. "What was she called?"

Her mum scratched her head. "It began with a K. Let me see . . ." She looked at the photo again. "Kihari!" she said suddenly. "That was it. She was about five years old."

Emily knew that elephant babies usually drank their mother's milk until they were about four, and then they stayed with their mums, living in a small group of females called a herd. She also knew that elephants were really sociable animals. They helped each other, liked to play and had very good memories. Emily looked at the photo of her and the elephant. "Is Kihari still alive?"

"I imagine so," her mum said. "Elephants usually live until they're about sixty-five, if nothing bad happens to them. We're going back to the same place where you met her last time. Maybe we'll see her!"

"I hope so," said Emily. She touched the elephant in the photo with one finger. Would the elephant still remember her? It was about eight years ago, so Kihari would be thirteen years old by now, but she knew elephants were never supposed to forget anything.

Kihari. She said the name in her head. She really hoped she would see her very first wild friend again!

For more fun, games
and wild stories, visit
wwf.org.uk/gowild